My Mum's Having a Baby!

Dori Hillestad Butler

Illustrated by
Carol Thompson

CAT'S Whiskers

For Cyndi and Ted D.H.B.
For Jane C.T.

This edition first published in 2006 by
Cat's Whiskers
Hachette Children's Books
338 Euston Road, London NW1 3BH

Cat's Whiskers Australia
Level 17/207 Kent Street
Sydney, NSW 2000

ISBN-10: 1 903012 74 0 / ISBN-13: 978 1 903012 74 1 (Hardback)
ISBN-10: 1 903012 75 9 / ISBN-13: 978 1 903012 75 8 (Paperback)

Published by arrangement with Albert Whitman & Company, Morton Grove, Illinois, USA
Text copyright © 2005 by Dori Hillestad Butler
Illustrations copyright © 2005 by Carol Thompson

A CIP catalogue record for this book is available from the British Library

Printed in China
10 9 8 7 6 5 4 3 2 1

19 May

Michael's Birthday!

from
Big
Sister!

Now there are four people in my family. There's my mum and dad and me

and . . .

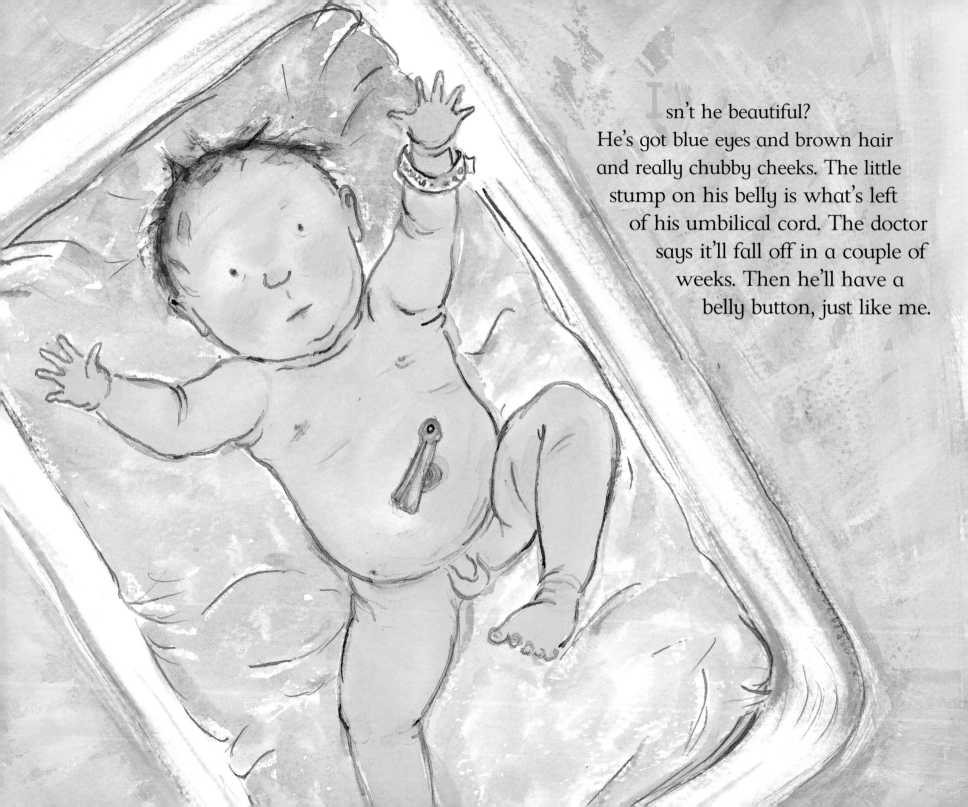

Isn't he beautiful?
He's got blue eyes and brown hair
and really chubby cheeks. The little
stump on his belly is what's left
of his umbilical cord. The doctor
says it'll fall off in a couple of
weeks. Then he'll have a
belly button, just like me.

Finally Dad calls us on the phone. Our baby is here!

It's hard work for my mum. That's why everyone says she's in labour right now.

It takes a long time to have a baby. First the cervix at the bottom of Mum's uterus has to open wide enough so our baby can get through. Then Mum has to push our baby down through her vagina and out between her legs.

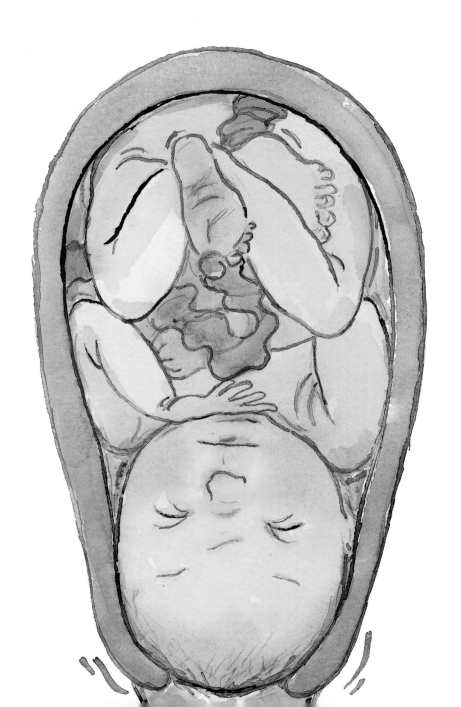

Dad rushes home from work and drives Mum to the hospital.

Grandma and I wait.   And wait.   And wait . . .

Two days after Grandma arrives, Mum shouts, "My waters have broken!" The water that protected our baby dribbles down Mum's leg and makes a puddle on the floor.

That means our baby is coming!

Mum starts to have contractions. Contractions are pains she gets in her belly when her uterus squeezes. All that squeezing helps our baby to get born.

Mum does some special breathing to help with the contractions.

May

In May, Grandma comes all the way from her house to stay with us. She's going to take care of me when Mum and Dad go to the hospital to have our baby.

I like it when Grandma comes. We make biscuits and play dominoes and just talk things over.

He's upside down!

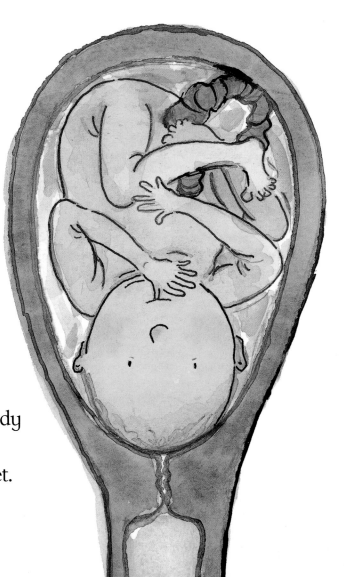

During March and April, our baby grows bigger and stronger. He doesn't have a lot of room to turn around any more. He settles low in Mum's uterus with his head pointed down. He's getting ready to be born.

Mum's belly is so big she can't even see her feet. She's tired a lot, and sometimes her back hurts.

Sometimes, when I lay my hand on Mum's big, round belly, I can feel him moving. The hard bump is where his head is. I like to rub his head gently and say, "Nice baby!" I think he likes it, too.

Nice baby!

February

It's February now and our baby is as big as my toy rabbit. Guess what? He can hear! He can hear sounds inside Mum's body, like her heart beating and her stomach gurgling. He can also hear me talk and laugh and practise the piano. Sometimes, when he hears a loud noise, he jumps.

He can also open his eyes. There isn't much to see inside my mum, but he can tell the difference between light and dark.

Look! He's sucking his thumb!
Mum doesn't want to know yet whether our baby is a boy or a girl. She wants it to be a surprise when the baby is born.
Can't we just be surprised right now?

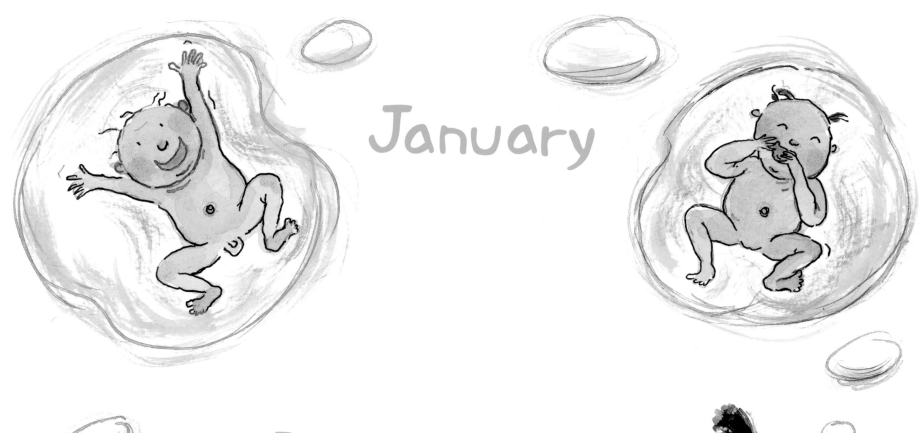

January

I wonder if our baby is a boy or a girl?
I hope he's a boy because we already have a girl
— ME! But I don't say it out loud.

We can find out if our baby is a boy when
we go with Mum to have her ultrasound.
Ultrasound lets us see our baby while he's still
inside my mum.

Pretty soon I'll be able to put my hand on Mum's belly and feel him, too. But I can't feel him yet.

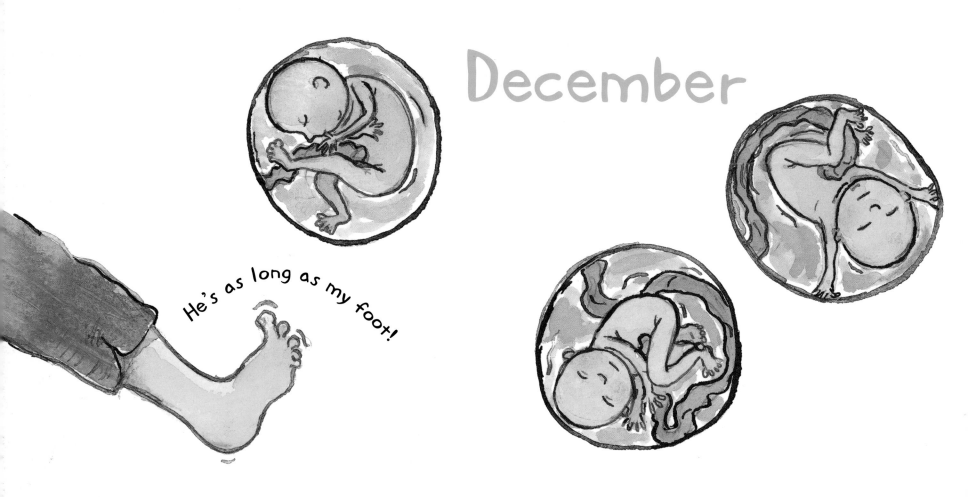

December

He's as long as my foot!

Our baby is growing bigger every day. Mum's belly s-t-r-e-t-c-h-e-s to make room. It's December and everyone now can tell there's a baby inside her. Her belly bulges out a little.

Our baby is about as long as my foot. He can turn sideways and backwards and upside down. Sometimes Mum can feel him doing somersaults in there.

Dad's sperm (like tiny tadpoles!)

Mum's egg (the actual size is like a full stop at the end of a sentence)

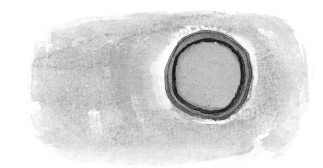

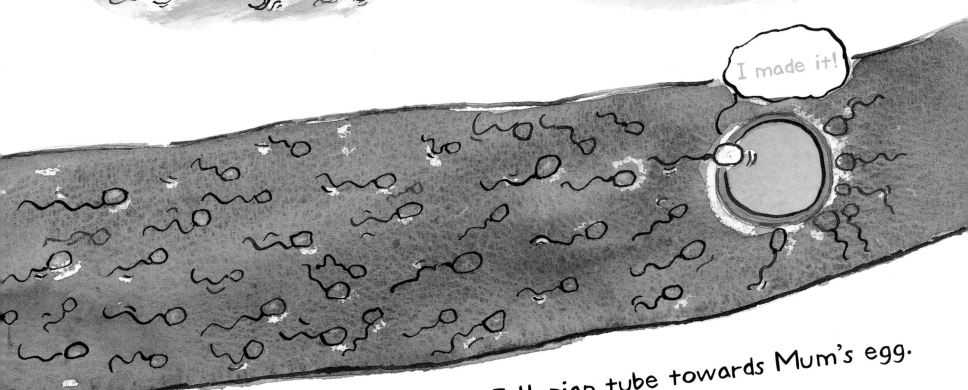

I made it!

The sperm swim like mad through a Fallopian tube towards Mum's egg. Only one sperm can join with the egg.

Mum says that when a man and a woman love each other so much that they want to make a baby, they lie really close to each other and hug and kiss. All this hugging and kissing feels nice. It makes the man and woman want to get even closer to each other.

The man puts his penis between the woman's legs and inside her vagina. After a while, a white liquid shoots out of the man's penis and into the woman's vagina. The liquid is full of millions of sperm. They swim up the woman's vagina, through her uterus and into one of her Fallopian tubes. If a sperm and an egg join together, nine months later a new baby will be born!

I wonder how our baby got inside my mum. One day, she and I have a nice talk about that.

Mum says it takes two people to make a baby: a man and a woman. Children can't make babies.

Tiny sperm are made inside a man's testicles. Tiny eggs are stored inside a woman's ovaries. A sperm and an egg must join to make a baby.

When a sperm and an egg come together, in a place called a Fallopian tube, we say the egg is "fertilised". The fertilised egg moves down the Fallopian tube and into the uterus. There, all snug and safe, it grows into a baby.

But how do the sperm and the egg get together, I wonder?

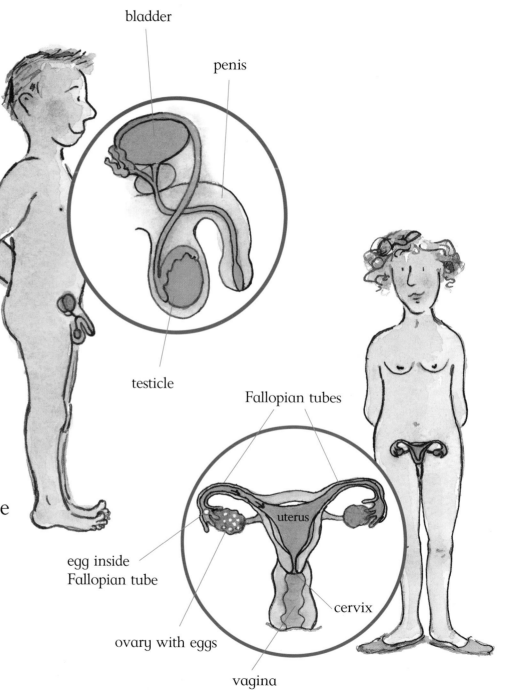

bladder

penis

testicle

Fallopian tubes

uterus

egg inside
Fallopian tube

cervix

ovary with eggs

vagina

It's November now and our baby is twelve weeks old. All his body parts are formed, but he's only as big as my index finger. He has soft nails on his fingers and toes, eyelids that are shut tight, and twenty teeny, tiny buds inside his mouth that will become his teeth.

November

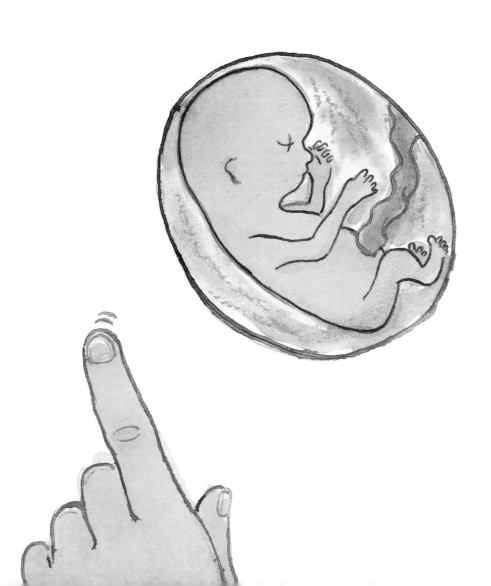

The doctor weighs Mum and measures her belly. Then she puts a special instrument on her belly so we can hear our baby's heart beating. It's loud and fast. It sounds like a galloping horse!

Mum has to go to the doctor a lot to make sure both she and our baby stay healthy. Sometimes she feels really sick, but the doctor says that's normal because of all the changes going on in her body. Mum says she'll feel better soon.

The food my mum eats travels from her bloodstream through the umbilical cord, too. I think that's a brilliant way to eat broccoli, but it's not such a good way to eat ice cream.

October

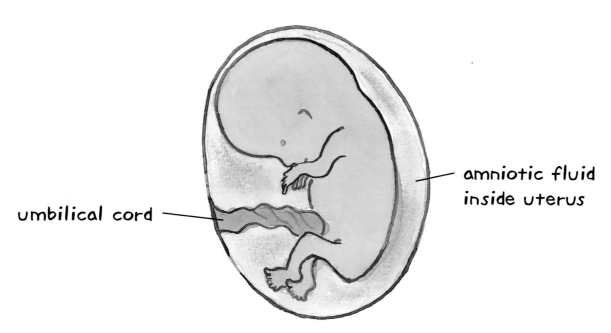

umbilical cord

amniotic fluid
inside uterus

Mum's uterus is like a balloon that grows bigger and
bigger. Our baby is nice and cosy in there. He's not too hot and
not too cold. He's surrounded by warm water called amniotic
fluid. The water protects him so he doesn't get bumped around
too much.

It's October now, and our baby has eyes, ears, fingers
and toes. He can't breathe by himself yet. He gets all the
oxygen he needs through a twisty tube called the umbilical cord.
The oxygen travels from Mum's bloodstream into our baby.

September

We've just found out about our baby, but he's been inside my mum for four weeks. He's floating in a special place inside her belly called the uterus. He doesn't look much like a baby yet, but that's because he's only as big as my bottom front tooth. He already has a head, a backbone, and buds that will grow into arms and legs. He also has a heart that's already started beating.

It's September now, but he won't be born until May. That's a long time to wait.

Real size

baby

uterus

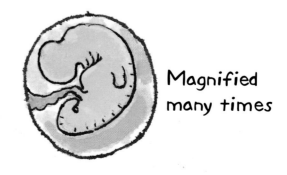

Magnified many times

Hi, I'm Elizabeth. Here I am with my mum and dad. You can't tell by looking at my mum, but there's a baby growing inside her. That baby is going to be my little brother or sister.